I0541137

FRAYLE

DEAD INSIDE

ALR021

Published by

Aqualamb

FRAYLE is
Gwyn Strang
Sean Bilovecky
Pat Ginley IV
Eric Mzik
Elliot Rosen

CREDITS:
Recorded & Mixed by Frayle
Mastered by Carl Saff @ Saff Mastering

All Songs written by FRAYLE
© FRAYLE All Rights Reserved
All lyrics written by FRAYLE and reprinted by permission

First Printing: Edition of 500
ISBN: 978-0-9985211-6-9

aqualamb.org

THANK YOU
Désirée Hanssen, Johnathan Swafford, Eric Palmerlee, Manuel Tinnemans
Thomas Haywood, Ram, Jon Paul Davis, John Strang, Jeannette Strang,
Karen Strang, Spike, Luna,Kyle Rose, Virginia Bilovecky, Nina Rose Bilovecky,
Marsha Craft, Evan Nolan, Mike Callahan, Frank Cavanaugh, Pat Ginley III,
JoAnne Ginley, Mckayla Ginley, Ryan Ginley, Katherine Mzik, Emmie Mzik,
Briar Golladay, Gunther Golladay

CONTENTS

The music for *Dead Inside*
can be downloaded
via the link below:

http://aqualamb.org/021

THIS IS A LIGHT I CAN'T SEE...

DEAD INSIDE

I FEEL DEAD INSIDE
SOMETIMES I HEAR THE ANGELS CRY
CALL ME TO THE WHITE LIGHT
I'M NOT DEAD YET, SO JUST LET ME LIE

I BLED OUT A LONG TIME
POISONED BY THIS PANTOMIME
TIRED OF WASTING TIME
SURRENDERED NOW TO THIS PAIN OF MINE

I LIE RESIGNED
I SEEK SALVATION
MY DARKENED MIND
AND HIS TEMPTATION

FRAGILITY, OLD FRIEND
I'M READY NOW FOR THIS PAIN TO END
TOO TIRED TO PRETEND
LET IT ALL GO AND LET IT TRANSCEND

I LIE RESIGNED
I SEEK SALVATION
MY BROKEN MIND
AND THIS FRUSTRATION

YOU ARE WORSHIPED
BY THE MOON,
AND WILL BE MOURNED
BY THE STARS.

FOR YOUR HEART HOLDS
BEAUTY WHERE MOST MEN
HOLD SCARS.

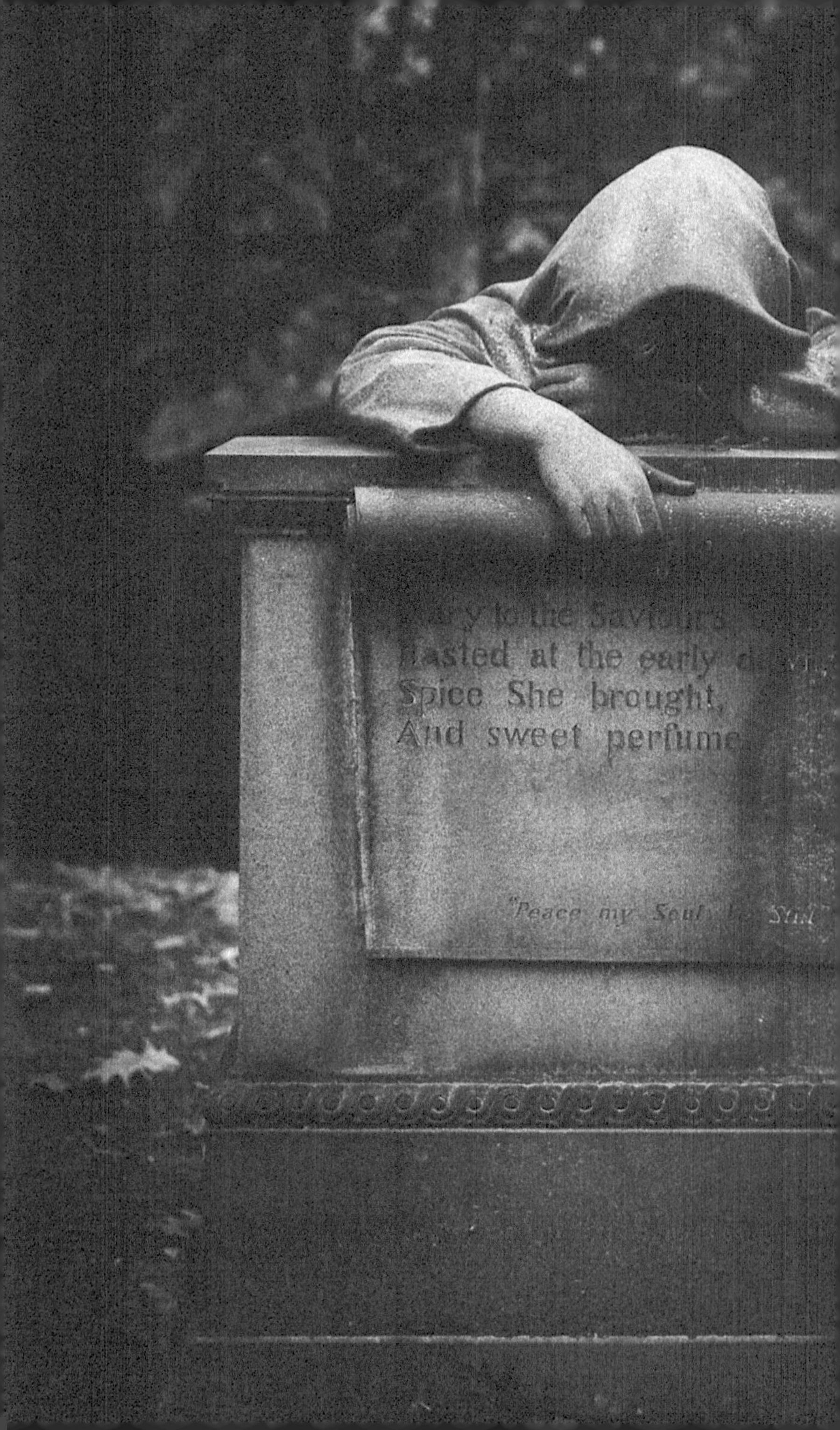
Hasted at the early
Spice She brought,
And sweet perfume

WE ARE OUR OWN GODS

GODLESS

WE BUILD TEMPLES TO WHAT IF'S
THOSE GHOSTS THAT LIVE IN YOUR HEAD
I'M NOT SO SURE IT'S A SIN
THOSE GHOSTS, THEY FILL ME WITH DREAD

CAN'T ALWAYS WALK AMONG THE PURE
CAN'T ALWAYS WALK AMONG THE BLESSED
SOMETIMES I FEEL SO INSECURE
SOMETIMES I FEEL GODLESS

WE'RE LIVING IN THE MUNDANE
LOOKING FOR LIFE IN GRAVESTONES
LIVING LIKE YOU HAVE NO CHOICE
YOU KNOW WE BUILD OUR OWN THRONES

CAN'T ALWAYS WALK AMONG THE PURE
CAN'T ALWAYS WALK AMONG THE DEAD
SOMETIMES I FEEL SO INSECURE
SOMETIMES I FEEL GODLESS

YOU LEAVE A BEAUTIFUL SCAR

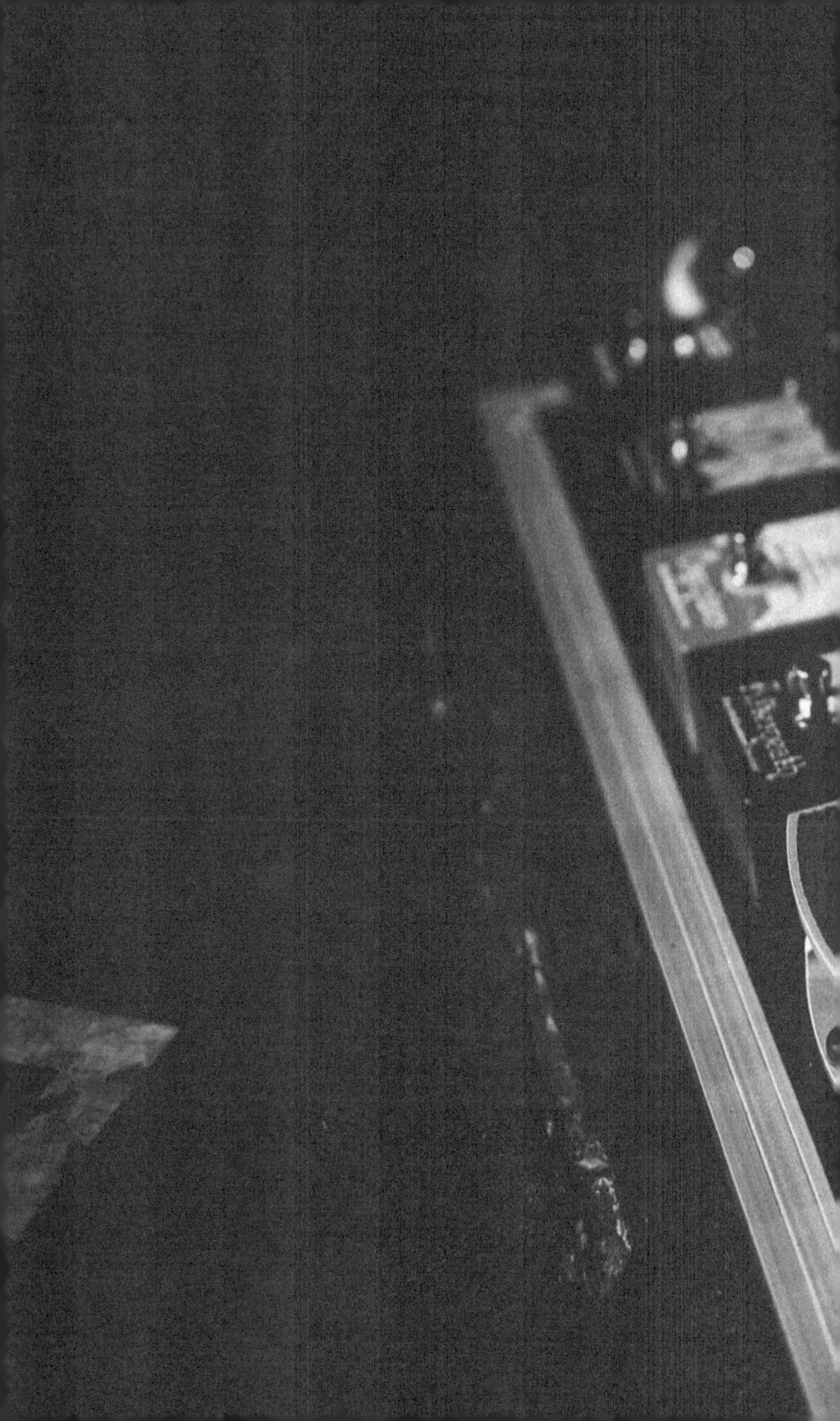

SEE MY FRAGILITY

DEMEAN ME

WASTE ME WITH YOUR LIES

LAY ME DOWN

WITHER INSIDE ME

AND LAUGH AT ME WHILE I CRY

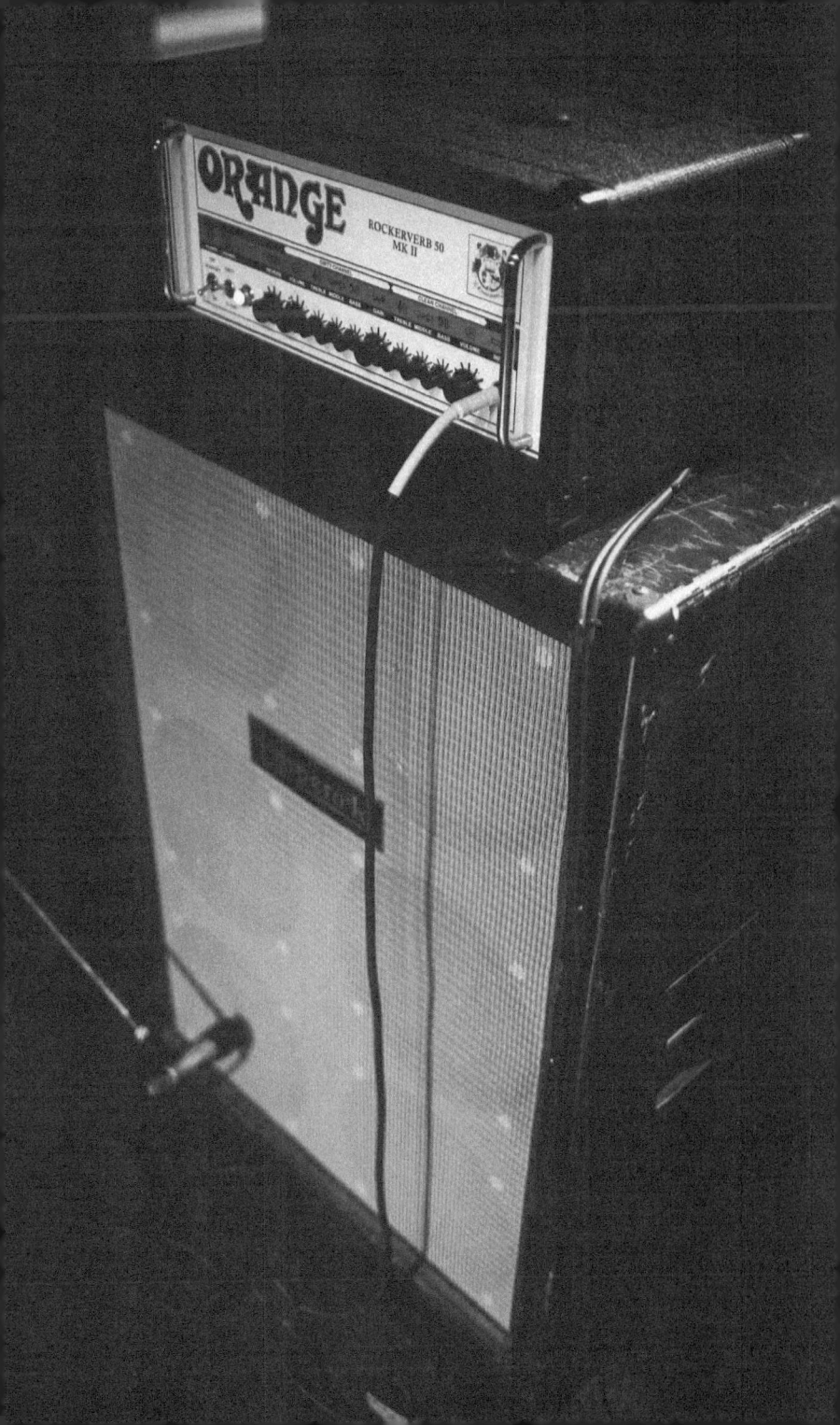

PROTECTION:

THRICE AROUND THE CIRCLE'S BOUND

EVIL SINK INTO THE GROUND

CHANGING SIN INTO GRACE.

@paul_verhagen_photo

As Above

___

So Below

@paul_verhagen_photo

@paul_verhagen_photo

@paul_verhagen_photo

@paul_verhagen_photo

HOLD ME DOWN

UNTIL I BELIEVE

ARISE, THE BROKEN.

@paul-verhagen_photo

THE LITTLE MONSTERS AT OUR DOOR

LAUGH AT US AND CALL US WHORES

TAKE AN AXE AND SPLIT THEIR HEAD

LAUGH AT THEM 'CAUSE NOW THEY'RE DEAD

LOVE:

BY THE POWER BELOW & ABOVE,

I AM ASKING THAT YOU BRING ME LOVE.

BY THIS SPELL THAT I HAVE CAST,

I WANT A LOVE THAT WILL ALWAYS LAST

RUN TOWARDS BEAUTY

EVEN IF IT'S AWAY

FROM THE LIGHT

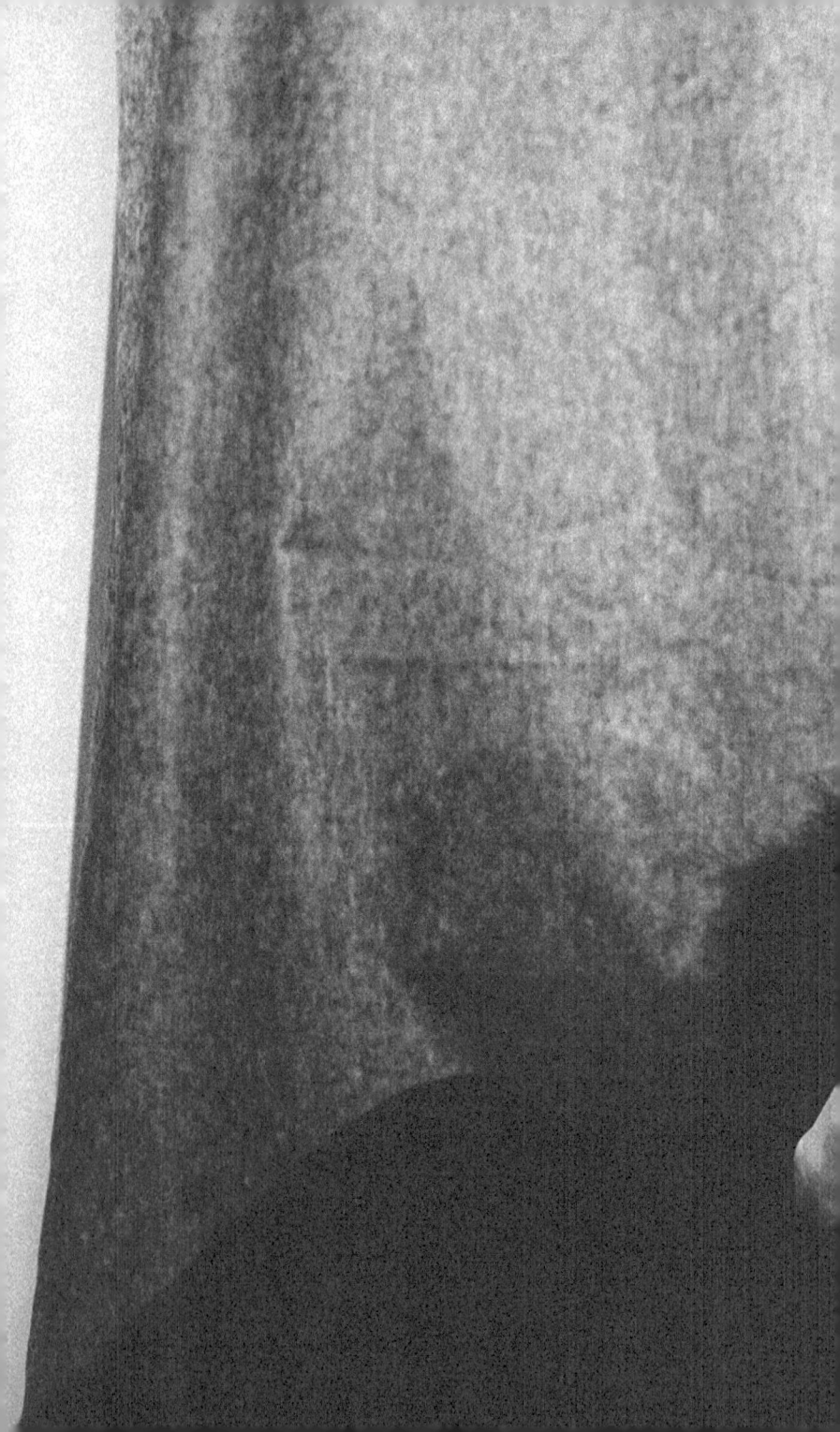

WE'RE ALL MADE

OF FIRE.

THE ONLY WAY

I KNOW HOW TO BREATHE

IS THROUGH YOU.

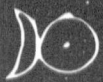

I'M THE ONE

WITH

NO SOUL

MISERY FEELS COMFORTABLE

NOW THAT YOU'RE GONE.

FAMILIAR LIKE A RAINY DAY.

TORTURE MYSELF

WITH THOUGHTS OF YOU.

WISH THAT YOU COULD HAVE STAYED.

7

PAIN

IS

THE

POINT

I PRAYED FOR RAIN

WHEN THE SUN WAS SHINING.

FOR S.

I KNOW I'VE KNOWN YOU IN A PAST LIFE.
I KNOW I'LL KNOW YOU IN ANOTHER.
I'LL CARRY YOU THROUGH, BABY
I'LL CARRY YOU THROUGH

A GIFT FROM GOD
BESTOWED UPON ME
OH, HOW I LOVE YOU
TO THIS DAY STILL
CAN'T TAKE IT AWAY FROM ME
CAN'T TAKE IT AWAY

THE LOOK IN YOUR EYES
SAID MORE THAN A THOUSAND WORDS
EVER COULD
I COULD GET LOST FOR A THOUSAND YEARS
IF ONLY YOU WERE THERE

MEMORIES FADE
BUT NOT YOURS
LIVE INSIDE ME FOREVER AND A DAY
JUST SAY YOU'LL BE WITH ME
JUST SAY YOU'LL BE THERE

SAME OLD STORY TOL

D A THOUSAND TIMES

☐ **DESCENDER by Descender** (ALR 001)
6 song debut EP. Available formats: Digipak CD, digital / streaming
90's Influenced post-hardcore. RIYL: Snapcase, Helmet, Quicksand
"Angularly aggressive hardcore that takes an abrasive shape on purpose." – CMJ

☐ **AND SO WE MARCHED by Descender** (ALR 002)
4 song EP. Available formats: Printed book, digital / streaming
90's Influenced post-hardcore. RIYL: Snapcase, Helmet, Quicksand
*"...a 21st Century compliant post-hardcore band that was raised on metal and got
dosed with a tab of AmRep..."* – Jaded Scenster

☐ **TAKING DRUGS TO MAKE MUSIC TO SELL CARS TO** (ALR 003)
by Human Highlight Reel
4 song debut EP. Available formats: Vinyl record, printed book, digital / streaming
Instrumental post-rock. RIYL: Maserati, June of 44, Russian Circles
"Aces instrumental post rock. Think Russian Circles or perhaps a more metal Seam..."
– Jaded Scenster

☐ **JUDGE by Vagina Panther** (ALR 004)
5 song EP. Available formats: Printed book, digital / streaming
Heavy female-fronted garage rock. RIYL: QOTSA, Cheeseburger, Fu Manchu, Stooges
"Vagina Panther rocks." – Billboard

☐ **BLACK BLACK BLACK by Black Black Black** (ALR 005)
12 song debut LP. Available formats: Vinyl record, printed book, digital / streaming
Melodic death rock. RIYL: Akimbo, Torche, Lungfish, Black Flag
*"Brooklyn-by-way-of-Ohio doomsters offer up a big, nasty salute to gas tanks and goat
hooves. It all coalesces to form one ravaging feast of melodic death rock that will satiate
all your salacious needs, be it Nether-deity worshiping or rock star living."* – Broken Beard

☐ **GODMAKER by Godmaker** (ALR 007)
4 song debut LP. Available formats: Vinyl record, printed book, digital / streaming
Doomy sludge metal. RIYL: High on Fire, Red Fang, Mastodon, The Sword
*"An example of genuine out of-nowhere brilliance. A patient drawn out campaign
of aggression."* – Relix

☐ **THE SPACE MERCHANTS by The Space Merchants** (ALR 008)
8 song debut LP. Available formats: Printed book, digital / streaming
Whiskey-soaked space-rock. RIYL: Black Mountain, Dead Meadow, The Besnard Lakes
*"A unique brand of lo-fi psych rock... their huge-yet-minimal sound, mixing psych with
blues and country style riffs to make something great."* – Magnet

☐ **HIRAM-MAXIM by Hiram-Maxim** (ALR 009)
4 song debut LP. Available formats: Vinyl record, printed book, digital / streaming
Noisy experimental doomgaze. RIYL: Swans, Suicide, Pink Floyd, Oxbow
*"Builds into an apocalyptic fervor before dissipating into a cloudy haze & ending before
you've had your fill."* – VICE

☐ **ALTERED STATES OF DEATH AND GRACE by Black Black Black** (ALR 010)
10 song sophomore LP. Available formats: Vinyl record, printed book, digital / streaming
Melodic death rock. RIYL: Akimbo, Torche, Lungfish, Black Flag
*"...the kind of good-natured misanthropy of bands like Whores or KEN mode, but the musical
gestures beneath the noisy exterior are all forward-charging, Kyuss-worshipping sludge n' roll.
It's basically underground metal's version of a radio banger."* – BrooklynVegan

☐ **TRESPASSES by Nathaniel Shannon & The Vanishing Twin** (ALR 011)
15 song debut LP. Available formats: Printed book, digital / streaming
Unsettling bedroom recording darkness. RIYL: Lanegan, Badalemnti, Springsteen, Waits
*"An unsettling yet captivating collection of songs compiled from a decade of bedroom
recordings... Shannon's spoken word-style vocals over haunting and minimalist
instrumentals lend a creepy atmosphere to the record."* – Decibel

☐ **FERA by Husbandry** (ALR 012)
8 song debut LP. Available formats: Printed book, CD, digital / streaming
Female-fronted math rock meets post-hardcore. RIYL: Mars Volta, Glassjaw, Refused, Deftones

"It's hard to believe that Husbandry is not the biggest band in the world. They're heavy and mathy, chaos wrapped in hard rock and heavy metal." – Nerdist

☐ **MURDEREDMAN by MURDEREDMAN** (ALR 013)
8 song sophomore LP. Available formats: Vinyl record, printed book, digital / streaming
Post-punk inspired noise rock. RIYL: Savages, Bauhaus, Boris, Killing Joke

"A patient and disciplined examination of anxiety and melancholy underpinned with a cathartic tension-and-release structure that borrows from goth, post-metal, and no-wave..." – New Noise Magazine

☐ **IN TENSIONS by Lo-Pan** (ALR 014)
5 song EP. Available formats: Vinyl record, printed book, CD, digital / streaming
Anthemic desert rock. RIYL: Soundgarden, ASG, Torche, Red Fang

"Calling Lo-Pan a stoner band is a disservice to the amalgam of influences the band successfully merges together: the soulful alt rock of the 90s with a thundering doom/sludge sound that's equal parts immediate and timeless." – Nine Circles

☐ **GHOSTS by Hiram-Maxim** (ALR 015)
7 song LP. Available formats: Vinyl record, printed book, digital / streaming
Noisy experimental doomgaze. RIYL: Swans, Suicide, Pink Floyd, Oxbow

"Everything is awash in mesmerizing ambient skree and squalls of atonal feedback. Think an extended, updated version of side 2 of Black Flag's My War." – Hellride Music

☐ **KISS THE DIRT by The Space Merchants** (ALR 016)
10 song sophomore LP. Available formats: Vinyl record, printed book, digital / streaming
Whiskey-soaked space-rock. RIYL: Black Mountain, Dead Meadow, The Besnard Lakes

"[T]he sonic equivalent of having an acid trip in the bathroom between Woodstock and a ZZ Top concert in '69" – New Noise Magazine

☐ **BAD WEEDS NEVER DIE by Husbandry** (ALR 017)
5 song EP. Available formats: Printed book, CD, digital / streaming
Female-fronted math rock meets post-hardcore. RIYL: Mars Volta, Glassjaw, Refused, Deftones

"While retaining their bold go-anywhere style, the EP is a more streamlined and focused effort, signaling a greater maturity and command of recording." – Echoes and Dust

☐ **BY THE GRACE OF BLOOD AND GUTS by Haan** (ALR 018)
8 song LP. Available formats: Printed book, Vinyl, CD, digital / streaming
Noise, Grime, Sludge, Metal, Rock. RIYL: Unsane, Melvins, Swans, Helmet, Clutch

"If Melvins and Unsane had a kid while under the influence of hallucinogens" – Metal Insider

☐ **LUMINOUS VOLUMES by Skryptor** (ALR 019)
7 song LP. Available formats: Vinyl, Printed book, CD, digital / streaming
Noise, Math rock, Prog. RIYL: craw, Dazzling Killmen, Don Cabellero

"Galloping, off-kilter and unabashedly victorious, proggy noise-rock outfit Skryptor's takes hard-rock/psychedelic throwback tropes, flips them on their heads and stretches it all into an adventurous march through endlessly shifting soundscapes."" – Revolver

☐ **DEAD INSIDE by Frayle** (ALR 021)
7 song 7". Alchemy Box: Printed book, Vinyl, CD, digital / streaming
Heavy witch doom. RIYL: Chelsea Wolfe, Portis Head, Sleep, Sunn O)))

"Trades in dark psychedelics and heavy, dripping drums that punctuate the riffing that plays in and around vocalist Gywn Strang's superb voice." – Nine Circles

☐ **SUBTLE by Lo-Pan** (ALR 022)
11 song LP. Available formats: Vinyl, Printed book, CD, digital / streaming
Anthemic desert rock. RIYL: Soundgarden, ASG, Torche, Red Fang

Subtle was produced by James Brown (NIN, Foo Fighters, Ghost) and mastered by Ted Jensen (Mastodon, Deftones, Bad Company, GNR).

The music for *Dead Inside*
can be downloaded
via the link below:

http://aqualamb.org/021

www.ingramcontent.com/pod-product-compliance
Lightning Source LLC
Chambersburg PA
CBHW030237180626
46810CB00008B/3175